The

ıb

Nicola Davies
The Mountain Lamb

Illustrations Cathy Fisher
GRAFFEG

The Mountain Lamb

It was the smallest lamb Lolly had ever seen. She put it in her bobble hat and carried it down to shelter of the valley.

The stars were out by the time she got to the farmyard. Grandpa was in the barn, with all the other new born lambs and their mothers. Gently, he took the lamb from Lolly and looked it over.

'Never seen such a little scrap!' he laughed. 'Reminds me of you when you were born! Where d'you find her, Lol?'

Lolly didn't want to answer, but she didn't want to tell Grandpa a lie either.

'Up on the moor,' she said.

'Hmm,' said Grandpa. 'You know your gran doesn't like you going up there alone.' Grandpa frowned. His blue eyes always went ice-coloured when he was cross, and they were doing that now. Lolly looked down at her boots.

'Yes, Grandpa.'

'But you did right to bring an orphan lamb in, where we can give her a chance.'

Grandpa stopped frowning. His eyes thawed a bit and he plonked Lolly's hat on her head with one hand so it slid over one eye.

'Better not tell your gran that you've been carrying sheep in your new hat!'

Lolly reached up and stroked the lamb, lying peacefully in the crook of Grandpa's arm. She could feel the tiny ribs beneath the silky nubble of baby wool.

'Grandpa,' she said. 'Can I keep her, for my own? Bottle-feed her and all?'

'It's hard work, Lol, a lamb's not a toy!'

Grandpa was frowning again now, eyes cooling. But Lolly was determined. She stuck her chin out and held her grandfather's wintry stare.

'I know about rearing lambs and I don't mind the work.'

Grandpa sighed. 'Hmmmm,' he said. 'Well... I don't know...'

The lamb scrunched her eyes shut and snuggled her head into Lolly's warm palm.

'Please, Grandpa, please. She's like me. She's little and she's lost her mum.'

Lolly looked up into Grandpa's eyes. They'd melted now to the colour of a summer sea.

'All right, my Lol,' he said quietly. 'But don't set your heart on her, she's very weak. If I can get her through tonight, she's yours. Now run along in and get your tea.'

The farmyard seemed full of starlight as Lolly ran to the kitchen door. She *knew* her lamb was going to live. She just *knew* it!

Lolly woke when it was still dark. She could hear her gran in the kitchen below, clattering the big kettle onto the range and tinkling the cups into their saucers, ready for breakfast. Usually Lolly jumped straight out of bed, but this morning she wriggled back under the blankets. She wasn't so sure about her lamb now. She remembered the fragile ribs, the tiny nuzzling head. 'Weak,' Grandpa had said. 'If I can get her through the night,' he'd said. *If.*

Lolly curled up small and pulled her pillow over her head. She didn't want to go downstairs to hear bad news.

Thump, thump, thump. Gran was banging the kitchen ceiling, Lolly's bedroom floor, with the broom handle to call her down for breakfast. Lolly threw back the covers and scrambled into her clothes. You didn't wait for Gran to call you twice!

'Porridge is poured,' said Gran, nodding her head to the table, where three full bowls sat under their little clouds of steam. Lolly slid into her chair just as Grandpa came in from washing his hands in the scullery. She wanted, more than anything, to ask about the lamb, but she was afraid of what she'd hear.

Grandpa sat down. 'Mmmmm,' he said, 'your gran's porridge is hotter than the molten magma at the centre of the Earth.' He picked up his spoon and began to eat. Lolly searched her grandpa's face for clues about the lamb.

His cheeks were red and polished from the cold air, but he looked tired. Was that a good sign or a bad one? She didn't know.

'C'mon, my Lol,' said Grandpa, smiling. 'Tuck in. Get some of that magma heat into you on this frosty morning!'

Grandpa was being very jolly. He must be trying to cheer her up. That was most definitely a very bad sign. Lolly spread soft brown sugar over the surface of her porridge. At first it looked like sand, but in moments it melted into little pools and rivulets. Lolly pushed them with her spoon. She didn't feel like eating.

Gran sat down and poured them each a cup of tea.

'That's yours, Lolly,' she said.

'Yes, drink up now,' said Grandpa. 'You'll need all your strength today.'

What did he mean? Lolly blew on her tea and looked at her gran and then at her grandpa. Gran's face was flat and empty, as it always was these days, but Grandpa seemed to be holding back a smile. Lolly couldn't work it out.

Then, she heard a tiny bleat. It came from a cardboard box tucked between the wall and the range. Lolly had been so busy expecting the worst news that she hadn't looked out for signs of the best.

'Maiiirrr! Maaiirr!' said the lamb. Her voice was too small to be loud, but it was very definitely demanding. Grandpa grinned.

'Madam wants her breakfast. You better see to it, Lol,' he said. 'She's worse about being kept waiting than your gran. Bottle's ready by the range.'

Lolly had bottle-fed lambs many times before, but she'd never seen one so eager for her feed. This lamb planted her four feet, not much larger than pencil ends, and squared up to the bottle as if she was going to fight it! Even though her mouth was barely big enough to go around the teat, she sucked so hard that Lolly had to grip the bottle tight with both hands. The level of milk dropped fast and the lamb's small stomach swelled visibly. As it did, her tail began to wiggle, faster and faster, until it was just a blur and Lolly had got the giggles. Gran and Grandpa both left the breakfast table to watch.

'I haven't heard you laugh like that in a long time, Lolly!' said Grandpa, and he looked at Gran and nodded.

'So,' he said. 'What are you going to call her?'

Lolly looked at the wiry little body, so tough in spite of its size, and without thinking any more about it she said, 'Susan. I'm going to call her Susan.'

No one had said that name aloud for months. Suddenly the kitchen seemed very quiet indeed. Grandpa put his hand on Gran's shoulder, but she shrugged him off.

'The washing up isn't going to do itself,' she said, and a

moment later she was at the sink, clattering dishes into the bowl with the radio turned up loud.

'That's a good name,' Grandpa said gently. 'I've always liked it. That's why we gave it to your mum.' Then he put his boots back on and went out to the yard. Lolly took Susan in her arms and stroked her head until she fell asleep.

Grandpa had been right. Rearing a lamb was hard work. Especially a lamb like Susan. She bleated for her food four or even five times a day. Each time, Lolly had to wash out the bottles and teats and make up the feed from powdered milk and water. Susan butted Lolly's shins impatiently whilst she a waited for her bottle, and jumped up so her sharp little hooves poked into Lolly's legs. She didn't like being left alone either. As soon as she was strong enough to jump out of the box by the range, she began to follow Lolly everywhere, wriggling and squeezing her little bottom under gates and fences whenever she was shut in or left behind. Gran banned them from the house because Susan pooed on the floor, so Lolly and her lamb spent all day, every day, outside.

Lolly didn't mind a bit. Susan liked all the things that Lolly liked: playing chase, exploring, and making dens in the hay barn when it was too wet to be in the open. The lamb was such good company that Lolly would have slept with

her in her pen in the barn every night, if she'd been allowed.

Lolly knew that Susan wasn't really a pet, she was a farm sheep, and one day she'd be expected to join the flock and have lambs of her own. But every day Lolly pushed that thought to the back of her mind, and went out to play with Susan.

The days began to lengthen. Gran didn't have to rub the frost off the porch window anymore, and Grandpa stopped wearing his winter hat. Susan was eating hay and sheep nuts now, and only needed one feed of milk a day. She had a sturdy body, tough little black legs and she had grown too heavy for Lolly to carry.

'She's growing up fast!' Grandpa said one evening. He was leaning over the stable door, watching Lolly give Susan her last feed before bed.

'Another week or two and she won't need any milk at all...' Grandpa rubbed one hand through his hair, like he always did when he had something bad to say. 'So she'll be ready to go back with the flock, in time for you to go back to school.'

Lolly looked down at Susan's madly-waggling tail and at the last milk disappearing from the bottle.

'But she'll still need me,' she said quietly. 'Even when she's weaned.'

'What she needs most, Lol, love, is other sheep. Same as you need other children.'

Gran had marked the school terms and holidays on the calendar in the kitchen, even though Lolly hadn't been to school for months. Lolly watched the last few days of half term dripping away until it was the Monday morning that she was due to go back.

Lolly got up as soon as there was light to see with to tend to Susan before school. The lamb knew the sound of her footfalls and started to bleat as Lolly crossed the yard to the barn. Lolly gave her a little pail of nuts and scratched the tight woolly curls behind her ears as she ate her breakfast.

'Come on,' Lolly said. 'Let's go for a walk.'

It was cold and drizzly and a wet mist drifted down off the moor tops in straggles, like wool caught on barbed wire. It closed in behind them as they walked up the track, so that the farm disappeared and Lolly and Susan were all alone in a damp, grey world. Lolly sat down on a rock and Susan began nibbling Lolly's coat and then her hair. The lamb's delicate little lips sorted though the strands of wispy brown, tickling Lolly's scalp, so she began to giggle, in spite of herself. Grandpa was wrong – she didn't need other children, with their talking and their questions about her mum. Susan was all the company she needed. For a moment, Lolly thought she would just get up and walk off into the mist with the lamb. Then Gran's voice rang out through the stillness of the fog.

'Lolly! Lolly! Breakfast!'

She knew she had to try, because she'd promised Gran and Grandpa that she would.

Of course, the hardest part was leaving Susan. The lamb didn't want to be shut into her pen again so soon and she called out '*Maaiiiirrr!*' again and again.

'She'll be just fine,' Grandpa said. 'I'll introduce her to the flock this morning. You wait, by the time you get home she'll be skipping around with a load of friends. Just like you will!'

Lolly tried to smile, but found she was biting her lip instead.

'Time to go!' Gran said. 'Up you hop!' Gran opened the door of the Land Rover and Lolly climbed aboard.

Lolly hadn't been off the farm in months and months. The village was just down the hill, but school and other children were all part of the life she had lived with her mother. Now, that life seemed as distant as another planet. Lolly couldn't imagine herself in any part of it.

Lolly was glad today that Gran didn't chat, like she used to when Mum was alive. They travelled down the hill in silence. She was glad, too, that the fog got thick. It covered up the houses and the gardens that had once been so familiar, so she couldn't tell where she was.

Suddenly, a big lorry loomed out of nowhere and Gran

stopped to let it get past. For the first time, Lolly took her eyes off the road ahead and glanced to her left. There, just showing in the greyness, was a little red gate. The house it belonged to was invisible in the mist, but Lolly knew every detail about it. The scent of the roses that grew in its garden, the way the front door stuck in rainy weather, the creak of its landing floorboards under her mother's foot.

The lorry stopped moving, pinning the Land Rover where it was. Gran got out to see what was happening. Lolly got out too and stood in front of the gate. She wanted to push it open, the way she used to, and run up the path to find her mum, back from a trip, brown and skinny, unloading her pack onto the kitchen floor. But she couldn't even touch it; the memories she felt would burn her hand.

Instead, she walked to the front of the lorry to find Gran. Grandpa's truck was parked in the middle of the road. And there was Susan, running about, with Gran, Grandpa and the lorry driver trying to catch her. She ran between their legs to Lolly, bleating delightedly. Lolly knelt down and buried her face in the soft coat, and when she told them she wanted to go back to the farm, nobody said a word.

Spring green crept slowly up the hillsides, colouring the hedgerows and fields and spreading at last up and over the moor. Grandpa's sheep dotted the pastures grazing in the sunshine but Lolly's lamb wanted nothing to do with them. She wanted to go exploring with Lolly or, sometimes, on her own.

She'd learnt, on the morning Lolly tried to go to school, that she could jump out of her pen, and now there was hardly a fence or a hedge on the whole farm that could hold her. She went where she pleased.

'She's a mountain goat, not a sheep!' Grandpa laughed. He didn't seem to mind about Susan wandering all over the place. But Gran did. Susan had twice got into Gran's flower garden. The first time she ate all the primroses and the second time she trampled the snowdrops.

'If that animal gets into my garden once more, I will eat her with mint sauce!' Gran said.

'I think she means it,' Grandpa whispered. So he spent a whole morning putting two strands of barbed wire on top of the garden fence to keep Susan out. That didn't seem to please Gran either.

'It looks like a prison camp!' she said, and went back inside.

Susan spent the night in the yard outside the kitchen door but she woke every morning at four, and *baaed* for attention. Grandpa always got up at five, but Lolly knew he needed his last hour of sleep, so Susan could not be left to bleat until everyone was awake. Lolly had to get up every morning and feed her. It was a good thing nobody mentioned school anymore, because by nine o'clock Lolly needed a nap!

Gran didn't want Lolly 'running wild', so she had to do chores: housework with Gran in the morning and farm work with Grandpa in the afternoon.

The mornings were difficult. Lolly and Gran used to have lots of giggles over the housework, but now they didn't know what to say to each other. Usually, they ended up working in different rooms, each of them quiet and alone.

The afternoons out with Grandpa were lovely. He liked having Lolly with him, now that Gran didn't come and help with the sheep like she used to. They walked miles over the pastures and moors. Lolly loved watching the two sheepdogs, Flinty and Megan, working the flock to Grandpa's commands.

'Away, away to me', 'come by, come by' and then, this mostly to Flinty, who was still very young and excitable, 'lie down, lie *down*'.

Susan came too, trotting along like another dog. Sometimes she was useful in encouraging warier sheep to do what Grandpa wanted. She'd go into a pen if there were

sheep nuts to tempt her, and the other sheep would feel safe to go in too, making the dogs' job much easier. But sometimes there were awkward moments, when Grandpa had said 'your lamb' twenty times in a row, to keep from saying 'Susan' even once.

Sometimes, Lolly and Grandpa would look round from some job with the sheep to find Susan had taken off. Grandpa said that she was just looking for some sheep she liked, but hadn't found the right ones yet. But Lolly worried and always went to look for her. Susan's boldness could get her into trouble.

Late one April afternoon, when the sky was gathering grey and the temperature was dropping, Susan vanished whilst Lolly and Grandpa were checking some fences.

'Leave her, Lol. She's probably run back down home. In with your gran's daffs, I'll bet!'

'I want to look for her, Grandpa.'

'We haven't got time, Lol. Got the vet coming to look at that ram in twenty minutes.'

'I can go on my own. She'll be stuck in the big bramble patch in the next field, like she was last time.'

It had taken Lolly an hour to get Susan out of that tangle and the lamb had lost a lump of fleece on the thorns.

'Alright, but if she's not there, promise you'll come straight back. Alright?'

Grandpa's eyes went pale and stern. 'It'll be dark in an hour, and I don't like the look of this sky.'

'I promise,' said Lolly, 'don't worry!'

Susan wasn't in the bramble patch in the next field, but Lolly was sure she'd be in her other favourite place, a thicket of gorse two fields higher, right on the edge of the moor. Grandpa had been right to worry about the weather.

Winter always had one last late fling up here, and now it looked like snow. Lolly knew how fast a blizzard could come down from the moor and drown you in blinding whiteness. You could freeze to death never knowing you were half a mile from home and safety. But that thought made her all the more determined to find Susan; she wasn't having her lamb out in a snowstorm overnight, even if it meant breaking her promise and taking a risk. Grandpa would do the same if he were missing a sheep.

Lolly looked into every hollow and dell of the thicket, all the places where the lamb had got herself stuck before. It took a lot of time, and when she looked up to check the weather again, her heart raced. The farm had gone, lost in a shroud of white that had spilled down from the moor on the other side of the valley. She looked behind her and saw that a blizzard was coming at her from above as well as below. If she ran down the field now it would catch her

in the open, where there was no shelter. Her only chance
was to hide from the storm, the way a sheep would, buried
in the heart of the thicket. She found a deep hollow full of
gorse bushes and crawled in amongst them. She hoped that
wherever Susan was, she knew enough to do the same.

Almost at once, the blizzard closed over Lolly's head, like
a vast falcon swooping on its prey. She heard the hit and
rush of the storm's wings above her, and felt the sudden
icy cold of its breath. Snow as fine as sand filled the air,
scouring every recognisable feature from sight. The white
of the snow and the black of the falling night mixed to a
swirling grey nothingness. Lolly crouched lower, hardly
feeling the stab of the gorse needles. She folded herself up
small, with her knees tucked into her coat and her hood
pulled tight over her head and face.

Lolly had never heard the wind make noises like it did in
that storm. It growled and shrieked around her so that she
imagined some monster getting ready to grab her. The cold
was intense. It sucked at her as she crouched in her spiny
hiding place, drawing the heat and life out of her no matter
how she resisted. She felt the blizzard wanting to kill her
and she was afraid, really afraid, for the first time in her life.

This was how her mother had died. Caught in a wicked
out-of-season storm high in the Himalayas. She'd fallen
almost two hundred feet. She had thought herself lucky to

be alive and crawled into her tiny tent, like a caterpillar in a cocoon, to wait whilst her partner went for help. But the storm had come: winds of a hundred miles an hour, blasts of ice particles like tiny razors in the air. Susan didn't give up. She fought. It took the storm three days to make her lie down and die.

'Never forget how much I love you', Susan had written on the last postcard she sent to Lolly. It got to the farm a week after the news of her death. It had a picture of smiling Sherpa on one side and Mum's big, loopy writing on the other. Lolly pushed it to the back of a drawer. She wanted to forget that love. So did Gran and Grandpa. Remembering it hurt too much. So Lolly tried to forget about her life with Mum in the cottage with the little red gate. That life was lost and gone, and without it the world was grey and empty.

Lolly could feel the cold taking her, creeping up her back and across her shoulders. It had got her legs and arms already, and was slithering into her belly and up through her chest. Soon it would take her heart. She felt sleepy.

She knew this was bad. It was the trick the cold played on you to tempt you to relax so it could kill you. That didn't seem to matter much now. Perhaps this was the best way of all to forget.

Quite suddenly, Lolly felt a sharp pain as gorse prickles stabbed her body through her clothes. The numbness in her

skin had gone, and now she was much too uncomfortable to sleep. Something inside her was pushing the cold back. A wave of warmth rolled up her tummy and lapped around her heart.

'Never forget how much I love you. Never ever, ever.' Her mother's voice whispered in her head, and then there was another voice calling, faint through the shrieking wind and then stronger.

'Lolly! Lolly!'

It was Gran!

A second later, Flinty was licking her face and barking fit to bust and a second after that there was a blinding torch beam and Gran scooping her up, easy as a newborn lamb.

'I never knew you were so strong, Gran.'

'Neither did I, my sweetheart. Neither did I.'

Lolly's lamb had come home on her own. Or not quite on her own. She'd hooked-up with the three wiliest old ewes on the farm, who lived high on the moor all year and only came down to shelter when the weather was at its worst.

'They walked into the yard as if was a hotel,' Grandpa said. 'Your lamb took them straight into the barn!'

Lolly's lamb and her new mates was a funny story now, in the safety of the morning, with the land all covered with a quiet silver blanket of snow. But last night it had told Grandpa that Lolly must be in danger.

'When I saw those three old girls, I knew we were in for a bad night. And I knew you'd stay out looking for that lamb, while she was safe in the barn!'

Gran and Grandpa had gone searching for Lolly as soon as the storm had struck. It had taken them almost four hours to find her.

'We called the Mountain Rescue,' said Gran, 'but they said it was too dangerous to be out on the moor.'

'That didn't put your grandmother off,' said Grandpa, 'she wasn't with the Mountain Rescue for nothing, you know.'

The Mountain Rescue! They only took really good mountaineers. Lolly remembered how pleased Mum had been when she had been accepted. She stared at her grandmother and then remembered to close her mouth. Gran laughed.

'I know, hard to believe to look at me now! But I did Mountain Rescue for twenty-five years.'

Grandpa reached across the table and squeezed his wife's hand. 'That's where your mum got her talent for climbing from, Lol.'

Gran's eyes filled up, but she kept her head high and took a deep breath. Then she spoke very slowly and carefully, as if she was pulling each word up from a deep well.

'Yes,' she said. 'I made Susan into a mountaineer.'

'And a fine mountaineer she was too,' said Grandpa.

Gran nodded her head and let the tears roll down her cheeks to the corners of her smile.

Lolly felt that her heart had just begun to beat again, after a long long time of lying still and frozen.

'Maaaiirr, maaiirrr.' A very familiar voice called from outside the kitchen door. Lolly's lamb had brought her three new best friends to get some extra breakfast.

The snow didn't thaw for ages. All the children in the village spent Easter tobogganing, so when Lolly stood up in front of her old class in school, she could see two arms in plaster and an obviously missing front tooth.

Lolly was giving a talk. She wasn't nervous because she'd practised it in front of Gran and Grandpa, and they'd really liked it. She had lots of things to remind her what to say: climbing ropes and rucksacks and photographs of her mum smiling at the top of mountains all over the world. She even felt OK when she got to the part about how her mum had died trying to climb a mountain. But the most important part of her talk came right at the end, and she had to take it very slowly.

'I'm glad my mum climbed mountains,' Lolly said, 'I'm very proud of her.' And then Lolly showed the class the postcard. She explained about Sherpas, and how they were the special mountaineers who helped people climb in the Himalayas. She read the words, in the loopy writing on the back, and she told her class how those words had kept her warm inside a blizzard.

'I will never forget how much my mum loved me. Not ever, ever, ever.'

Then Lolly sat down smiling, and everyone clapped.

Nicola Davies

Nicola is an award-winning author whose many books for children include *The Promise* (Green Earth Book Award 2015, CILIP Kate Greenaway Medal Shortlist 2015), *Tiny* (AAAS/Subaru SB&F Prize 2015), *A First Book of Nature*, *Whale Boy* (Blue Peter Book Awards Shortlist 2014), and the Heroes of the Wild series (Portsmouth Book Award 2014).

She graduated in Zoology, studied whales and bats and then worked for the BBC Natural History Unit. Underlying all Nicola's writing is the belief that a relationship with nature is essential to every human being, and that now, more than ever, we need to renew that relationship.

Nicola's children's books from Graffeg include *Perfect* (2017 CILIP Kate Greenaway Medal Longlist), *The Pond* (2018 CILIP Kate Greenaway Medal Longlist), the Shadows and Light series, *The Word Bird, Animal Surprises* and *Into the Blue.*

Cathy Fisher

Cathy Fisher grew up with eight brothers and sisters, playing in the fields overlooking Bath.

She has been a teacher and practising artist all her life, living and working in the UK, Seychelles and Australia.

Art is Cathy's first language. As a young child she scribbled on the walls of her bedroom and ever since has felt a sense of urgency to paint and draw stories which she feels need to be heard and expressed.

Cathy's first published books with Graffeg include *Perfect*, followed by *The Pond*, written by Nicola Davies. Both books were Longlisted for the CILIP Kate Greenaway Medal.

Country Tales series by Nicola Davies

Flying Free
Nicola Davies
Illustrations by Cathy Fisher

The Little Mistake
Nicola Davies
Illustrations by Cathy Fisher

The Mountain Lamb
Nicola Davies
Illustrations by Cathy Fisher

A Boy's Best Friend
Nicola Davies
Illustrations by Cathy Fisher

Pretend Cows
Nicola Davies
Illustrations by Cathy Fisher

Spikes and Sam
Nicola Davies
Illustrations by Cathy Fisher

Visit our website author pages www.graffeg.com for more about the author Nicola Davies and illustrator Cathy Fisher, plus a complete list of our children's books and merchandise.

Graffeg Children's Books

Perfect
Nicola Davies
Illustrations by Cathy Fisher

The Pond
Nicola Davies
Illustrations by Cathy Fisher

The White Hare
Nicola Davies
Illustrated by Anastasia Izlesou

Mother Cary's Butter Knife
Nicola Davies
Illustrations by Anja Uhren

Elias Martin
Nicola Davies
Illustrations by Fran Shum

The Selkie's Mate
Nicola Davies
Illustrations by Claire Jenkins

Bee Boy and the Moonflowers
Nicola Davies
Illustrations by Max Low

The Eel Question
Nicola Davies
Illustrations by Beth Holland

The Mountain Lamb
Published in Great Britain in 2019
by Graffeg Limited

Written by Nicola Davies
copyright © 2019.
Illustrated by Cathy Fisher
copyright © 2019.
Designed and produced by Graffeg
Limited copyright © 2019.

Graffeg Limited, 24 Stradey Park
Business Centre, Mwrwg Road,
Llangennech, Llanelli, Carmarthenshire
SA14 8YP Wales UK
Tel 01554 824000 www.graffeg.com

ISBN 9781912654109

1 2 3 4 5 6 7 8 9